To Dylan, our Little Chef
—M. S. & E. W.

A FEIWEL AND FRIENDS BOOK

An imprint of Macmillan Publishing Group, LLC

175 Fifth Avenue, New York, NY 10010

LITTLE CHEF. Text copyright © 2018 by Matt Stine and Elisabeth Weinberg. Illustrations copyright © 2018 by Paige Keiser.

All rights reserved. Printed in China by RR Donnelley Asia Printing Solutions Ltd., Dongguan City, Guangdong Province.

Our books may be purchased in bulk for promotional, educational, or business use. Please contact your
local bookseller or the Macmillan Corporate and Premium Sales Department at (800) 221-7945 ext. 5442
or by e-mail at MacmillanSpecialMarkets@macmillan.com.

Library of Congress Cataloging-in-Publication Data

Names: Weinberg, Elisabeth, author. | Stine, Matt, author. | Keiser, Paige, illustrator.

Title: Little Chef / Elisabeth Weinberg & Matt Stine ; illustrated by Paige Keiser.

Description: First edition. | New York : Feiwel and Friends, 2018. | "A Feiwel and Friends book"—Title page verso. | Summary: In honor of the special day, Lizzie
wakes up super early, as any good chef should, to prepare the perfect meal for her grandmother, whom Lizzie lauds as the greatest chef in the world.

Identifiers: LCCN 2017041734 | ISBN 9781250091697 (hardcover)

Subjects: | CYAC: Cooks—Fiction. | Cooking—Fiction. | Grandmothers—Fiction.

Classification: LCC PZ7.1.W4317 Li 2018 | DDC [E]—dc23

LC record available at https://lccn.loc.gov/2017041734

Book design by April Ward

Feiwel and Friends logo designed by Filomena Tuosto

First edition, 2018

1 3 5 7 9 10 8 6 4 2

mackids.com

Little Chef

ACHOOOooooo

Matt Stine & Elisabeth Weinberg

Illustrated by Paige Keiser

Feiwel and Friends • New York

Hello, my name is Lizzie.

And I am a chef.

Ever since
I was a baby,
I loved to cook.

My mom and dad
call me their Little Chef.

I have my own special hat and coat made just for me!

Chefs have to wake up early and stay up late. This morning
I woke up Mom and Dad extra early because it's a very
special day. . . . Grandma is coming over for dinner!

My grandma is the greatest chef in the world. She taught me everything I know. Today I'm going to cook a perfect dinner for her! My grandma expects the best.

On a special day like today, I need to have a big breakfast!
I'm making my famous scrambled eggs. First, I crack the
eggs in the bowl and mix them up with a fork.

Then I pour in some salt and pepper.
That's called seasoning. To be a great chef,
you need to season your food just right.

After a delicious breakfast, Mom and I write a list of all the ingredients we need for dinner. Tonight I am going to make Grandma's Super Special Smashed Sweet Potatoes. I want to show Grandma that I can cook just like her.

A chef always gets the best ingredients, and that means going to my favorite place . . .

We get to the market early so I can get the freshest fruits and vegetables.

Grandma and I love sweet potatoes! They are better than regular potatoes because they're a cool orange color and sweet like candy! I pick out the best ones I can find.

We buy a fuzzy peach
even though it's not on the
shopping list. I get to eat it
right there in the market.

Once we get home, it's time to start cooking! I tell Mom we should begin with the sweet potatoes.

Mom and Dad peel and chop them and get them ready for me.

stir... stir... stir...

Do you know the best part about making Smashed Sweet Potatoes?

Smashing them!

Now it's time to add the secret ingredient! Grandma says every great recipe has one. It makes a chef's food taste extra special and delicious.

STOMP! STOMP! STOMP! STOMP!

Oh no! The secret ingredient isn't in the recipe!

Now my sweet potatoes will never be as good as Grandma's!

I guess I'll have to find my own secret ingredient. I'll look in the spice cabinet—maybe I can find one in there!

How about this one? Nope, too spicy! Grandma won't like any of these! Hmmm . . . What am I going to do?

ACHOOoooooo

Of course! This is the
perfect secret ingredient
for my sweet potatoes.
Grandma will love this!

Thump!
Thump!
Thump!

Finally, it's time to take a taste! A chef has to
taste everything to make sure it's perfect—
and my grandma expects the best.

Grandma is here!

I can't wait for her to see what I've made!

Now we are ready for my favorite time of day. . . .

Dinnertime!

Daddy takes the first taste: "Mmm!"
Then Mommy takes a taste: "Mmmm!"
Finally, Grandma takes a taste.

"Delicious!" says Grandma. "These are even **BETTER** than my own Super Special Smashed Sweet Potatoes. What's your secret ingredient?"

"Grandma, you know a chef never tells **ANYONE** her secret ingredient!"

"What a perfect meal," says Grandma.
"And being with you is the best
ingredient of all."

"You did it again, Little Chef," says Mom.
"Now off to bed," says Dad.

Before I go to sleep, I have just one question. . . .

What should I cook tomorrow?

Chef Lizzie's (Grandma's) Super Special Smashed Sweet Potatoes

Serves 4 (plus one hungry dog)

Tell your parents to take you to the market to go food shopping.
Here is your shopping list:

3 medium-size sweet potatoes (about 2 pounds)
¼ teaspoon salt
1 SECRET INGREDIENT (Choose your own secret ingredient.
Every Little Chef has one! The spice cabinet is a good place to look!
Spices are what chefs use to make their food taste extra special.)

STEP ONE:

Pick out the best sweet potatoes that you can find. No brown or soft spots . . . gross!

STEP TWO:

Tell Mom or Dad to wash the sweet potatoes, peel them, and chop them into big chunks.
Make sure your helpers do a good job. A chef expects the BEST!

STEP THREE:

See that cool orange color? The potatoes are ready to be cooked! Ask your parents to
drop them into a pot of boiling water . . . and don't get too close! The water is HOT!

STEP FOUR:

After 20 minutes, it's time for the chef to test the potatoes to see if they are done. Have Mom or Dad take a fork and poke the sweet potatoes. Be careful not to touch them with your fingers—they're hot! If they are soft and mushy, then they are ready! Ask Mom or Dad to drain the sweet potatoes, shake off any extra water, and put them in a big mixing bowl.

STEP FIVE:

It's time for every Little Chef's favorite part . . . SMASHING THE POTATOES! This step is the most important and the MOST FUN! Smash the sweet potatoes with a potato masher or a big fork until they are smooth with no big lumps.

STEP SIX:

Add the salt and a dash of your SECRET INGREDIENT to the bowl and stir. Remember, a little chef never tells their Secret Ingredient!

STEP SEVEN:

Take a taste to make sure it's seasoned just right. A chef always tastes first.

And that's it.
Chef Lizzie's Super Special
Smashed Sweet Potatoes
are ready!